King Wilbur the Third and his lovely Queen were looking
at their Royal Palace. It was a sad sight. Everything
was broken down or falling down and they had no money for
repairs.

"Isn't it a terrible mess?" the King said.

"It is," the Queen sighed, "but what can we do?"

Wilbur shook his head. "Just look at it. Walls
falling down, doors broken and a garden full of weeds.
And the fountain in the courtyard hasn't worked for years."

The King and Queen walked carefully through the tall
weeds to the Royal Stables.

"Even my horse is getting old," Wilbur said as they
went inside.

The Queen patted the old horse gently. "He's rather
nice though," she said.

"Of course he's nice," Wilbur said as he gave the horse
a lump of sugar. "It's just that he's old."

"Anyway he shouldn't
have to pull that thing,"
Wilbur added pointing
to the Royal Coach. "I've
seen better milk carts."

The Queen smiled. "It
was a milk cart, Willy,
don't you remember?"

Wilbur nodded.

"Wouldn't it be lovely
if we had a new one," the
Queen said.

"Mm," the King said as
they left the Stable.

As they walked back to the Palace, Wilbur pointed to the flag flying on the flagpole.

"Huh," he said, "we haven't even got a decent flag."

"We certainly need a new flag," the Queen said. "We also need some new furniture and carpets and curtains. But we haven't any money."

"Then we must find some," the King said. Suddenly he turned and marched into the Palace. The Queen followed. He strode into his office and stopped in front of the big iron safe. Bending down, he put the key in the lock and opened the door.

"There!" Wilbur shouted as he lifted a box from inside. "We'll sell the Crown Jewels. We'll sell them all and make this the finest Royal Palace in the world. We'll have servants, guards, horses, new furniture and carpets."

"And a warm bathroom," added the Queen, "with lots of hot water."

Wilbur laughed. "Of course we'll have a new bathroom."

"And some new curtains," the Queen said.

"New curtains, new clothes . . . even a new flag."

The following morning, the King took the box of jewels, climbed on his old horse and set off. He rode on and on, selling a jewel here and a jewel there until he had sold them all.

One week later Wilbur returned to the Palace. He was
tired but happy as he put the money in the safe.

Then the King and Queen began to plan. The Queen
chose new carpets and curtains while the King sent for
the best workmen in his Kingdom.

When the King had found
the workmen, he ordered
some of them to rebuild the
Palace walls. He told
others to make new doors
and windows. One man made
a flagpole to put on one of
the tall towers.

Then the King set the
men to work inside the
Palace. There were lots
of jobs to be done.
There were stairs and
chairs to mend.

There were doors that
would not open and doors
that would not shut.
Everything went well until
Wilbur began to help.
 The trouble started
while Wilbur and the Queen
were having lunch.
 Suddenly they heard a loud
bang outside the dining room.
 "What's that noise?"
the King shouted.

Then he turned and looked towards the doorway.

"It's only someone working," the Queen replied.

"I know," the King said, "but it's lunch time . . ."

Suddenly the noise grew louder. Wilbur jumped up from his chair and ran across the hallway into the Throne Room.

"What are you doing making all that noise?" he shouted.

An old servant was kneeling in front of the huge fireplace with ropes and sticks. The King's own guard was standing beside him.

"Push and pull," the guard cried, "push and pull."

"Push and pull what?" exclaimed Wilbur. "What on earth are you doing?"

"Your Majesty," the servant replied, "I was trying to sweep the chimney, but the brush is stuck."

Wilbur strode towards the fireplace.

"Jerk it," he ordered.

"I have, Your Majesty, but nothing happens."

The King took hold of the brush handle and jerked it hard. There was a roar as soot fell down in a great cloud. It covered them all from head to toe.

Wilbur looked at them. "There," he said, "that's how you sweep a chimney." And then he stormed out of the room.

It was a long time before Wilbur came out of the bathroom. He was clean but not very happy. It had taken ages to fill the bath because the water trickled so slowly from the taps.

At the top of the stairs he met the Queen.

"Do you like it, Willy?" she asked, as she pointed to the carpet that two men were laying.

He smiled, nodded and then walked downstairs and out into the courtyard. Outside, he checked that everything was going according to plan. Suddenly he looked up. "The fools," he cried, "they've put my flag upside down!" He hurried into the Palace and ran upstairs.

"Careful, Your Majesty," called one of the workmen. "The carpet isn't fastened down yet."

Wilbur took no notice. He ran up the stairs until he was within three steps of the top. Suddenly the carpet began to slip and the King fell. He grabbed the end of the carpet as he tried to save himself but he began to roll. He rolled faster and faster, pulling the carpet with him. "Help!" he cried . . . but no one could help.

By the time he reached the bottom of the staircase Wilbur felt quite ill.

The Queen and the two workmen unrolled the carpet as quickly as they could, which made him feel terribly dizzy. They helped him to his feet and he tottered away towards his office.

He went inside, hoping to find a comfortable chair.
Then he stopped. Two painters were working there. They
were standing on a long plank set on two tall ladders.
They were painting the ceiling.

"Stop," the King shouted. "It's all wrong. You're
using the wrong colour!"

Wilbur's sudden shout startled the painter nearest
the doorway. He turned to see who was there,
slipped and fell off the plank. The tin of paint
shot out of his hand and flew high into the air.
Then it hit the ceiling, turned upside down . . .

. . . and fell on Wilbur. In a second he was white . . .
completely white . . . from head to toe. The painter lying on
the floor was covered in white paint too.

Wilbur walked sadly to the bathroom. This time
it took him even longer to get clean.

By the time Wilbur had washed off all the paint he was feeling much better. He walked carefully down the stairs and out into the courtyard. He checked to make sure his flag was now the right way up. It was, but the fountain was still not working. Before he could find a workman to ask him about it, he heard a noise at the main gateway. It came from a hundred men who were running into the courtyard. They were all shapes and sizes. These were the men from whom Wilbur was to choose the new Royal Guards.

"Line up by the wall!" the King shouted.

The men did as they were told. Then Wilbur looked at each man in turn. Some were big, some were small, some were fat, some were thin. Once again Wilbur walked along the line looking at each man.

Then he stopped and thought hard. Big guards cost

more to feed than small ones, but they would look better
on parade.

Wilbur chose the six biggest and sent the others home.
For the next two hours he taught the new guards how to
stand, march, turn and salute. At last he was satisfied.

Just then he saw the Queen looking out from an upstairs
window. He waved. Then suddenly water shot up from the
fountain. Someone, somewhere had turned it on. The
water went high into the air and came down like a
waterfall . . . on to the King.

He shouted and roared, but no one switched it off. He was drenched.

It had been a hard day for Wilbur. He'd been black, he'd been white, he'd been bumped downstairs rolled up in a carpet, and now he was wet . . . very wet. He dripped his way towards the Palace door. The Queen was standing there waiting for him. She was trying not to smile.

The King looked again at the fountain. He saw that it was now sending out little jets of water, just as it should. He turned towards the Queen and began to laugh. He laughed and laughed and laughed.

"You'd better have another hot bath, Willy," the Queen said as they walked inside the Palace. "Why don't you use the new bathroom?"

Wilbur ran up the stairs and stopped at the top. Then he turned and looked around him. Maybe he had had a bad day, but the Palace was almost finished.

"I hope it's sausages for supper," he called as he went into the bathroom.